Holiday in Catland

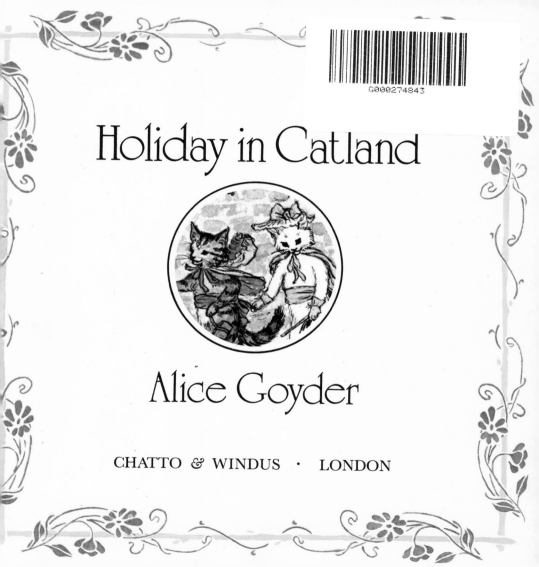

Alice Goyder

CHATTO & WINDUS · LONDON

Holidays! Mother Grimalkin was taking Tilly and Minnie to the seaside. Aunt Tabby was going too. The old leather trunk was filled to bursting with toys and books and clothes.

At the station it was all hustle and bustle and slam and clatter. Tilly held very tightly to Mother Grimalkin's hand.

When they arrived, there was a neat, trim carriage to meet them. Tilly and Minnie could already scent a whiff of the sea in the air.

Tilly and Minnie wanted to rush down to the beach straight away but Mother Grimalkin was very firm. After such a long journey she wanted her tea!

Near the beach was a shop full of kites and toy boats and all kinds of exciting treasures. Tilly and Minnie bought buckets and spades.

The beach at last! How soft and warm and slithery the sand was! Tilly made Minnie a fine feather bed all out of golden sand.

Next morning Tilly and Minnie went for a ride along the shore all by themselves in a cart pulled by two nanny goats.

In the afternoon they hunted for mussels in the rock pools at the edge of the sea, all amongst the slippery seaweed and scuttling crabs.

Old Mr. Shanty took Tilly and Minnie
for a row round the bay in his fishing boat
and Tilly tried to catch a jelly-fish.

In the evening they strolled by the bandstand on the promenade until sleep began to tug at their eyelids.

The swishing murmur of the waves lapping
the shore lulled Tilly and Minnie into
a sleep as deep as the deep, blue sea.

Published by
Chatto and Windus Ltd
40 William IV Street, London WC2N 4DF

Clarke, Irwin & Co Ltd, Toronto

Edited, designed and produced by
Culford Books
135 Culford Road, London N1

First published 1978

ISBN 0 7011 2348 6

Printed and bound by
Waterlow (Dunstable) Ltd, England